Reina

the

Cat

Inspired By True Events

Rachel Vasquez-Price / Jenny Raney

This book is dedicated to Alexis, Zachary, Brandon, and Kendra.
A special thanks to my son Steven for making this book a reality.

Outskirts Press, Inc.
http://www.outskirtspress.com

ISBN: 978-1-4327-8054-8

Outskirts Press and the "OP" logo are trademarks belonging to Outskirts Press, Inc.

PRINTED IN THE UNITED STATES OF AMERICA

My name is Reina, and this is my story.

When I was born, my mother was unable to care for me. I was left in an empty room of a deserted house. I was lucky that a wonderful woman named Flora found me.

Flora volunteers at a local pet store that allows her to bring in stray dogs and cats, so they can be adopted. I was a bit frightened to have all those strangers handling me, when really all I wanted was something to eat and a nice warm place to curl up and sleep.

When Flora took me to the pet store, I was amazed at all the other kittens that were already there. She quickly put me in cage with two other newborn kittens that were peacefully sleeping. It was great at last to be in a warm and secure place. All the employees at the pet store were very accommodating. They fed us every day and made sure our litter box was clean and that we had fresh water to drink.

I was only a few weeks old, so I slept most of the time. During the daylight hours when the pet store was open for business, there were many children with their parents. Some would ask Flora if they could pick us up and pet us. I often wished they would take me home with them, because I loved being petted and stroked, but no one seemed to be interested, and soon I would be placed back into my cage.

One day a nice-looking woman with gray hair walked into the pet store and asked Flora if she could hold me for a few minutes. She told Flora that her name was Rachel, and she was interested in purchasing two kittens. She explained how much she loved cats and had always had a cat at home while growing up. She was now retired, so she had the time to care of a small calico kitten like me. She liked the color of my coat, which had patches of white, orange, and black. I instantly loved her. She had a soft voice and stroked me very lovingly. I then heard her say that she wanted to buy another kitten so I would not be lonely and cry at night when she brought me to her house. That news was terrific! It was turning out to be a great living arrangement.

Rachel then went to get her son Steven, who had been busy looking to buy kitten food in the store, and asked him to select the second kitten. Steven then chose a cute little dark tortoiseshell kitten. Tortoiseshell cats have coats with patches of red, black, and brown. Steven quickly named him Zippy, because he was constantly jumping playfully over the other kittens in his cage.

When we arrived at our new home, Zippy and I were a little frightened, until we realized how much Steven loved animals. He loved us so much that he insisted that we sleep in his bedroom in a box with warm blankets. Zippy and I both knew we were the luckiest kittens in the world to have been adopted by two people who really loved us.

The next day Rachel decided to name me Reina. For some unknown reason, I favored Rachel, and Zippy just wanted to be held by Steven. As we grew older, I spent most of my time on Rachel's bed. I always made sure one of my paws touched her as she quietly read books. Now and then she would take time to stroke my head.

Zippy almost always liked to be on Steven's lap while he worked at his computer and often rode around on Steven's shoulders. Zippy loved to chase me around the house and jump over me when I was busy eating. It was a great deal of fun to play with him.

As the days turned to weeks and then months, we grew bigger and stronger. One day Rachel said, "I think Reina and Zippy are now a year old and should be able to go out to explore the outside world."

Zippy and I were excited. It was a little bit scary at first, but we couldn't wait to see how it felt to roam freely and discover the outside world. We climbed trees and fences, chased squirrels, and met other neighborhood cats. We found it to be a peaceful neighborhood with just a few fenced-in dogs that we soon learned to stay away from.

Every morning Rachel fed us and let us go outside, and then every evening, she called us to come back into the house. I would hear her voice and then I come running to go inside. Zippy, on the other hand, refused to go inside unless Steven called for him. Steven would give out a loud whistle, and then—and only then—would Zippy run into the house.

The next three years flew by fast. Zippy and I thought we had a perfect life, but as everyone knows, life is rarely perfect. On one very hot summer day, Rachel looked out her patio window and saw what looked like a black bag.

As she looked more closely, she realized it was Zippy, and he was not moving. He just lay motionless on the patio. She called for Steven, and he confirmed her worst fears; Zippy was dead. He showed no signs of foul play. No cuts or bruises were found on his body. It was a very sad day for all of us. We never found out what actually caused Zippy's death.

For the next few days, Rachel was afraid to let me play outside, but finally she relented, because I kept crying at the door to let me go outside. I had experienced what it was to run around and roam free and couldn't imagine not being permitted to go out. I was very careful to return home just before dark, and if I forgot, Rachel always remembered and called for me.

Another year went swiftly by, and then some more bad news. Rachel had been sneezing a lot and as a last resort went to an allergist. An allergist is a doctor who can tell you if you are allergic to something that is causing your body to have some negative reaction, such as sneezing, coughing, or body rashes. She quickly told the allergist that she knew she was not allergic to cats, because she had cats living with her all her life.

After taking a skin test, she was shocked to learn that she was highly allergic to cats. She couldn't believe it. Rachel then promised the allergist that she would use the nose spray he prescribed for her and try to limit her exposure to cats. She loved me so much, she knew she could not send me away. Since I wasn't allowed to stay inside the house during the day, she prepared a cozy box for me to sleep in the garage every night.

One evening in the summer month of June, I came to the back door so that Rachel would let me in as usual. To my surprise, she did not open the door. No matter how loudly I cried out, no one would open the door to let me in.

I was a little confused, but I was happy to stay out in the cool summer night. It was all very unusual. I returned that evening, and still no one was home to let me in. I looked into the sliding glass doors and could not see anyone or hear anyone.

I walked up and down the neighborhood, but still no sign of Rachel or Steven. Where had they all gone? I couldn't believe they had gone and left me all alone. For several nights I was not able to go into the garage to sleep in my cozy box. I slept in the empty doghouse that was kept in the back patio. Fortunately, every morning on an outside table, I found food in my dish and also fresh, clean water.

Finally one day after walking around the neighborhood, I heard Steven's voice calling me. I ran home but was surprised not to find Rachel. Steven just patted my head while I ate the food he had put out for me. He looked sad, but always seemed to be in a hurry, so he quickly left me. Again, no one was home to let me in. This routine went on for several days, and then one day I saw strangers inside the house. They were two girls, and Steven was helping them move in. When Steven and the two girls walked out to the patio to feed me, I overheard them say they were sorry to learn that Rachel had suddenly taken ill and had been rushed to the hospital. She had been stricken with a serious illness and would not be able to return home for a long time.

At last I knew why Rachel, who loved me so much, seemed to just disappear. Rachel was my best friend, and under normal circumstances, she would never have left me all alone . She could not send me away to live elsewhere, because both Steven and Rachel knew I never liked strangers to pet or even hold me.

Often Steven came to visit me. He made sure I always had food and water. Whenever I heard him calling me, I ran home as fast as I could. Because he often looked sad, I stayed close by and let him pick me up. I knew we both missed Rachel very much.

One day I saw a big van parked in the driveway. There were several people busy going in and out the house. Since the two girls were no longer living in the house, I wondered who those new people were. I then saw my friend Steven, and he looked very happy talking and giving directions to all of them. They helped get a passenger in a wheelchair out of the van. I ran to the back of the house, and when I looked into the sliding glass doors, I couldn't believe my eyes!

There sitting in a wheelchair looking out was my beloved friend, Rachel. When she saw me, her face lit up, and she called, "Hi, Reina. Hi, Reina. How is my little girl? Did you miss me? I missed you so much! I didn't abandon you. I was in the hospital all these months, but now I am back home again! I hoped and prayed that you would be safe."

It was one of the happiest days of my life. Rachel couldn't come out, so I just stayed by the sliding door, meowing and purring. I wanted to let her know how much I had missed her.

It was a wonderful surprise to see Rachel once again. I also had a surprise to share. A few weeks before, I had met a great playmate. He was a handsome red-haired domestic cat. His long, fluffy, silk-soft red fur made him look twice as big as he really was, and I decided to called him Rusty. When Rachel first saw him with me, she shooed him away, but then one day I heard Steven say, "Look, Mom, Reina has a new friend, and any friend of Reina's is a friend of mine." From that day on, my new best friend, Rusty, was always welcomed.

Every morning I walk up to the back sliding door where I can get a glimpse of Rachel in her wheelchair. I greet her with a soft meow, and then Rachel's caregiver, Myrna, comes out to feed us.

Rusty always lets me eat first. He waits patiently for his turn and never rushes me. We then take time to bathe ourselves. Keeping clean by licking our coats is our daily routine. We playfully chase each other all over the backyard. Rusty likes to play with my long tail as I swing it back and forth in front of his nose. Sometimes we chase birds or squirrels or capture grasshoppers, and then we usually curl up in one of Rachel's flower pots to take a nap in the sun together. One thing I have learned is that when you lose a best friend, you usually find another best friend.

CPSIA information can be obtained
at www.ICGtesting.com
Printed in the USA
258823LV00001B